CHARLIE BROWN
ALL TIED UP

Other *Peanuts* Kids' Collections

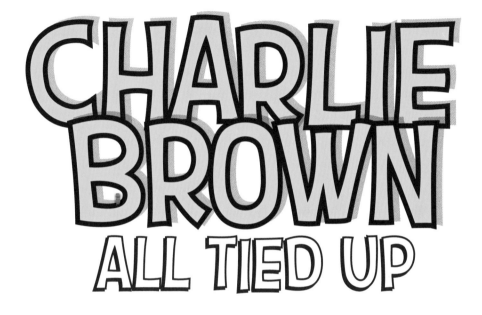

CHARLIE BROWN
ALL TIED UP

A PEANUTS™ Collection

CHARLES M. SCHULZ

Andrews McMeel
PUBLISHING®

↓

90

110

132

Make Your Own Miniature Kite!

MATERIALS NEEDED: 8.5 x 11 craft paper of different colors, safety scissors, extra-strength glue stick, pencil, ruler, paper straws (two for each kite), string or baker's twine, craft glue, ribbon or decorative string, glitter glue

INSTRUCTIONS:

1. Using two pieces of paper that can be different colors or patterns, fold the sheets in half on the longest edge so that the new size is 5.5 x 8.5. Use scissors to cut each piece of paper along the fold line.

2. With an extra-strength glue stick, glue one piece of paper to the back of the first one and smooth the page down.

3. Use a pencil to mark four dots on each side of the paper that will form the shape of your kite. The points at the top and bottom should be at the halfway mark across the page. The dots on the long edges should be about 3 inches down the page, measured from the top. Once you mark the dots, you can use a ruler to trace lines connecting them.

4. Cut out the shape of your kite with safety scissors.

5. Measure out about 24 inches of twine, and tie one end of the twine a third of the way down the paper straw. Add a drop of glue to secure the knot in place. The knot should be at the middle of the cross on the kite.

6. Cut the other paper straw into three pieces. Tie the opposite end of the twine to the middle of one of the paper straw pieces to make a kite handle. Add a drop of glue to keep the string from sliding off the handle.

7 Cut about 18 inches of lightweight ribbon or decorative string to make the kite tail. Tie one end of the string to the bottom of the longest straw, at the opposite end from the first knot. Add a drop of glue to secure the knot in place.

8 Decide which side you want to be the front (or top) of the kite, and lay it down so that the bottom of the kite is facing up.

9 Using a ruler and pencil, connect the corners of the kite to form a cross. Squeeze out a line of craft glue along the cross, and place the straws onto the glue to make the kite frame. Make sure the first knot of twine is at the center of the cross and the second knot is placed at the bottom of the kite. Let the glue dry for 5 minutes.

10 Decorate your kite with glitter glue or draw fun faces and designs with markers. Tie some short ribbons along the kite tail for decoration.

Now your kite is ready to fly. Just watch out for that evil kite-eating tree!

*As a variation of this project, use pasta noodles instead of paper straws. Or, make the kite size smaller and use tissue paper to make kites that you can hang in the window for decoration. Have fun!

Make an Edible Woodstock's Nest

   With an adult's help, make this sweet treat for you and your friends to enjoy.

INGREDIENTS: 1 5-oz. can of chow mein noodles; 1 12-oz. package of chocolate chips; 1 bag of small jelly beans; peanut butter (or alternative cashew or almond butter); wax paper; paper plates. (Makes about 15 nests.)

INSTRUCTIONS:

1. Put a piece of wax paper on each plate.

2. Put chow mein noodles in a large bowl.

3. Melt chocolate chips in the microwave or over low heat on the stove.

4. Pour chocolate over noodles and mix.

5. Place a heaping tablespoonful of the mixture on the wax paper on each plate. Have an adult test to see when it's cool enough to form the mixture into nests.

6. Stick the jelly beans down with peanut butter inside the nest.

Charles M. Schulz and *Peanuts* Fun Facts

- Charles Schulz drew 17,897 comic strips throughout his career.

- Schulz was first published in Ripley's newspaper feature *Believe It or Not* in 1937. He was fifteen years old and the drawing was of the family dog.

- From birth, comics played a large role in Schulz's life. At just two days old, an uncle nicknamed Schulz "Sparky" after the horse Spark Plug from the *Barney Google* comic strip. And that's what he was called for the rest of his life.

- In a bit of foreshadowing, Schulz's kindergarten teacher told him, "Someday, Charles, you're going to be an artist."

- Growing up, Schulz had a black-and-white dog that later became the inspiration for Snoopy—the same dog that Schulz drew for Ripley's *Believe It or Not*. The dog's name was Spike.

- Charles Schulz earned a star on the Hollywood Walk of Fame in 1996.

Andrews McMeel Publishing
a division of Andrews McMeel Universal
1130 Walnut Street, Kansas City, Missouri 64106

www.andrewsmcmeel.com

www.peanuts.com

19 20 21 22 23 SDB 10 9 8 7 6 5 4 3 2 1

ISBN: 978-1-5248-5226-9

Library of Congress Control Number: 2019932570

Made by:
Shenzhen Donnelley Printing Company Ltd.
Address and location of manufacturer:
No. 47, Wuhe Nan Road, Bantian Ind. Zone,
Shenzhen China, 518129
1st Printing—7/22/19

ATTENTION: SCHOOLS AND BUSINESSES
Andrews McMeel books are available at quantity discounts with bulk purchase for educational, business, or sales promotional use. For information, please e-mail the Andrews McMeel Publishing Special Sales Department: specialsales@amuniversal.com.

Check out more *Peanuts* kids' collections from Andrews McMeel Publishing.